EEK & ACK

ACK'S NEW PET

written by
BLAKE A. HOENA

illustrations by
STEVE HARPSTER

STONE ARCH BOOKS
a capstone imprint

Eek and Ack Early Chapter Books
is published by Stone Arch Books,
A Capstone Imprint
1710 Roe Crest Drive
North Mankato, Minnesota 56003
www.capstonepub.com

Library of Congress Cataloging-in-Publication Data
Hoena, B. A., author.
  Ack's new pet / by Blake A. Hoena; illustrated by Steve Harpster.
    pages cm. -- (Eek and Ack: early chapter books)
  Summary: Eek decides to make his brother Ack a pet out of snottle
bugs.
ISBN 978-1-4342-6406-0 (hardcover)
ISBN 978-1-4342-6551-7 (paperback)
ISBN 978-1-4342-9232-2 (ebook)
  1. Extraterrestrial beings—Juvenile fiction. 2. Brothers—Juvenile
fiction. 3. Pets—Juvenile fiction. [1. Extraterrestrial beings—Fiction.
2. Brothers—Fiction. 3. Pets—Fiction. 4. Science fiction.] I. Harpster,
Steve, illustrator. II. Title.
  PZ7.H67127Ac 2014
  813.6—dc23   2013027858

Printed in China by Nordica.
1013/CA21301916
092013   007743NORDS14

TABLE OF CONTENTS

Chapter 1

ACK IS BORED

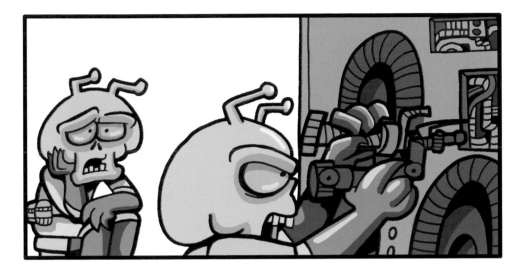

As Eek worked on his spaceship, Ack looked sad.

"What's wrong?" Eek asked.

"I'm bored," Ack replied.

"You could help me," Eek said. "Then we could go conquer Earth."

"No way!" Ack said. "The last time we tried that, we got sucked into a black hole."

"But nothing bad happened," Eek said.

"It felt like we were flushed down a toilet," Ack said. "I was sick for a week!"

"Fine," Eek grumbled. "What do you want to do?"

"Hmm," Ack thought for a moment. "I want a pet."

"Like a pet earthling?" Eek asked.

"No, no. I want a pet we can teach to do tricks," Ack said. "Like to sit or fetch comets."

"Yeah, earthlings aren't smart enough to learn tricks like that," Eek said.

"Do you think Mom would let us get one?" Ack asked.

"Probably not," Eek said. "She's still mad at us for breaking Dad's asteroid bowling trophy."

"Oh, yeah," Ack said. "We shouldn't have tested our rocket packs in the house."

Chapter 2

EEK HAS A PLAN

"I have a plan!" Eek said suddenly. Eek was always planning something.

"I hope this isn't another plan to conquer Earth," said Ack. "Those never work."

"No, and this plan will work," Eek said. "But first, what type of pet do you want?"

"You said Mom won't let us get a pet," Ack said.

"I don't plan on getting you a pet," Eek said. "I plan on making you one."

Ack wasn't sure what kind of pet he wanted.

"Three-eyed burplers are good at tricks," Eek said.

"Burplers are cool. How do you make one of those?" Ack asked.

"First, we drink lots of Solar Cola," Eek said. "Then we burp into a huge balloon, and—"

"But what if the balloon pops?" Ack asked. "I'm afraid of loud noises."

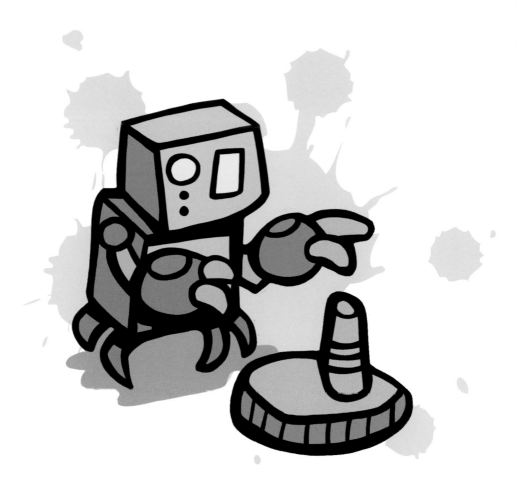

"Okay, would you like a robot?"
Eek asked. "I have some spare
parts from my spaceship."

"No, robots like to do
math," Ack said. "I'm afraid of
subtraction."

"That's silly!" Eek said. He shook his head. "How about a goober beetle instead?"

"No, no, never!" Ack yelled. He shook with fear. "I'm afraid of goober beetles!"

"Why?" Eek asked.

"I have one stuck up my nose," said Ack.

Eek looked up Ack's nose. "I don't see a thing," he said.

"Maybe it's gone now, but I still don't want one," Ack said.

"Fine," Eek said. "I'm going to
make you a pet that won't be loud,
do math, or get stuck up your nose.
Come on!"

Chapter 3

ACK GETS A PET

Eek and Ack zoomed around space, using rocket packs for power. Eek held on tight to a jar of snottle bugs.

"I caught another one!" Ack said.

"Put it in the jar," Eek said.

"Okay, but why are we catching all these snottle bugs?" Ack asked.

"I'll tell you later," Eek said. He flew off. "Just keep looking. We need about a million of them."

Finally the boys caught enough snottle bugs. Eek showed Ack his plan.

"I loaded my slimer with all of those snottle bugs," he said.

He started the slimer machine.
"When the bugs move through
my slimer, I'm going to squeeze
the snot out of the snottle
bugs," Eek said. "Your new pet
will plop out the other end of
the slimer!"

"Here it comes!" said Eek.

"He's getting bigger!" Ack shouted.

The pet hugged Ack's leg. "He likes me! He likes me!" Ack shouted.

"I think your new pet is sliming all over your leg," said Eek.

"That's a great name!" said Ack. "I think I'll call him Slimy!"

ABOUT THE AUTHOR

Blake A. Hoena once spent a whole weekend just watching his favorite science-fiction movies. Those movies made him wonder why those aliens, with their death rays and hyper-drives, couldn't actually conquer Earth. That's when he created Eek and Ack, who play at conquering Earth like earthling kids play at stopping bad guys. Blake has written more than twenty books for children, and currently lives in Minneapolis, Minnesota.

ABOUT THE ARTIST

Steve Harpster has loved to draw funny cartoons, mean monsters, and goofy gadgets since he was able to pick up a pencil. In first grade, he avoided writing assignments by working on the pictures for stories instead. Steve was able to land a job drawing funny pictures for books, and that's really what he's best at. Steve lives in Columbus, Ohio, with his wonderful wife, Karen, and their sheepdog, Doodle.

GLOSSARY

asteroid (ASS-tuh-roid)—a large space rock

black hole (BLAK HOHL)—an area in space that sucks in everything around it

comet (KOM-it)—a bright, heavenly body that develops a cloudy tail as it slowly moves around the sun in a long, slow path

conquer (KONG-kur)—to defeat and take control of an enemy; Eek always wants to conquer planet Earth.

earthling (URTH-leeng)—a creature from the planet Earth

grumbled (GRUHM-buhld)—complained about something in a grouchy way

snottle bug (SNOT-tuhl BUHG)—a slime-filled bug found on planet Gloop

three-eyed burpler (THREE EYED BURP-ler)—a lizard-like creature found on planet Gloop that is good at tricks

TALK ABOUT THE STORY

1. Eek and Ack are brothers. Do you think one of the alien brothers behaves better than the other? Explain your answer.

2. Do you think Eek and Ack's mom is going to let them keep Slimy? Why or why not?

3. Would you want Eek to make a pet for you?

WRITING TIME

1. Make up a pet of your own. Describe what it looks like and what things you can do with your pet.

2. Ack is afraid of goober beetles. Write about something you are afraid of.

3. Imagine that Eek and Ack got a pet that is found on Earth, like a dog or a cat. Write a story about them with their new Earth pet.

EXPLORING THE UNIVERSE

with Eek & Ack

Eek wanted to build Ack a pet robot, but Ack was afraid of the subtraction that the robot might want to do. Did you know that robots do a lot more than just math? Earthlings have been using robots to explore outer space for more than fifty years.

Robots first landed on the moon in 1966. The Surveyor spacecrafts were sent there to explore whether it was safe for earthlings to land on the moon. Some of these spacecrafts had robotic arms to test how soft the soil was.

In 1977, robots were sent to explore other planets. Voyager 1 and Voyager 2 flew by Jupiter, Saturn, Uranus, and Neptune. They took pictures of the planets.

THE *FUN* DOESN'T STOP HERE!

DISCOVER MORE AT...
www.CAPSTONEKIDS.com

FIND COOL WEBSITES AND MORE
BOOKS LIKE THIS ONE AT WWW.FACTHOUND.COM.
JUST TYPE IN THE BOOK ID: 9781434264060
AND YOU'RE READY TO GO!